Purchased from
Multnomah County Library
Title Wave Used Bookstore
216 NE Knott St, Portland, OR
503-988-5021

What is Wrong With Our Mom?

Helping Children Understand Bipolar Disorder

 *SAND AND SEA BOOKS*

What is Wrong With Our Mom?

Helping Children Understand Bipolar Disorder

By Adele Marie Luttrell   Illustrated by Jeff Vernon

Copyright 2008 by Adele Marie Luttrell

All rights reserved. No part of this publication may be reproduced, stored in a retrieval system or transmitted in any form or by any means, electronic, mechanical, photocopying, recording or otherwise, without the written permission of the Publisher.

SAND AND SEA BOOKS

www.sandandseabooks.com   email: adele@sandandseabooks.com

3858 Bluff Street
Torrance, CA 90505, USA
Tel: 310-528-8139

Library of Congress-In-Publication Data
    Luttrell, Adele Marie, 1957-
    What Is Wrong With Our Mom/by Adele Marie Luttrell
    Illustrated by Jeff Vernon -- 1st Edition

Summary: Helps children to understand the mental illness, "bipolar disorder" while offering hope that there is help available for those afflicted with this disorder.

Ages 6-12

ISBN: 978-0-9788964-16 (Softbound)
ISBN: 978-0-9788964-23 (Hardbound)

The Library of Congress No. 2008932742

...nuture the child...heal the world...

My brother Jack and I live with our Aunt Cheryl.
Our Dad lives far away and our Mom is not well.
She has a kind of sickness that is hard to see
because it is in her mind, not her body.
We had to move in with Aunt Cheryl
because Mom is sick.

For a long time Jack and I did not understand what was wrong with our Mom.
She looks like all the other Moms.
She is pretty with long brown hair and warm eyes.
She has soft hands and smells pretty.
When Mom smiles at us we feel loved, happy and safe.

But sometimes she looks angry and says mean things. Other times she ignores us and we wonder, "Did we do something wrong?"

Some days our Mom does not get out of bed even when we tell her we have to go to school.
She says, "I'll be right there."
But she still doesn't get up!

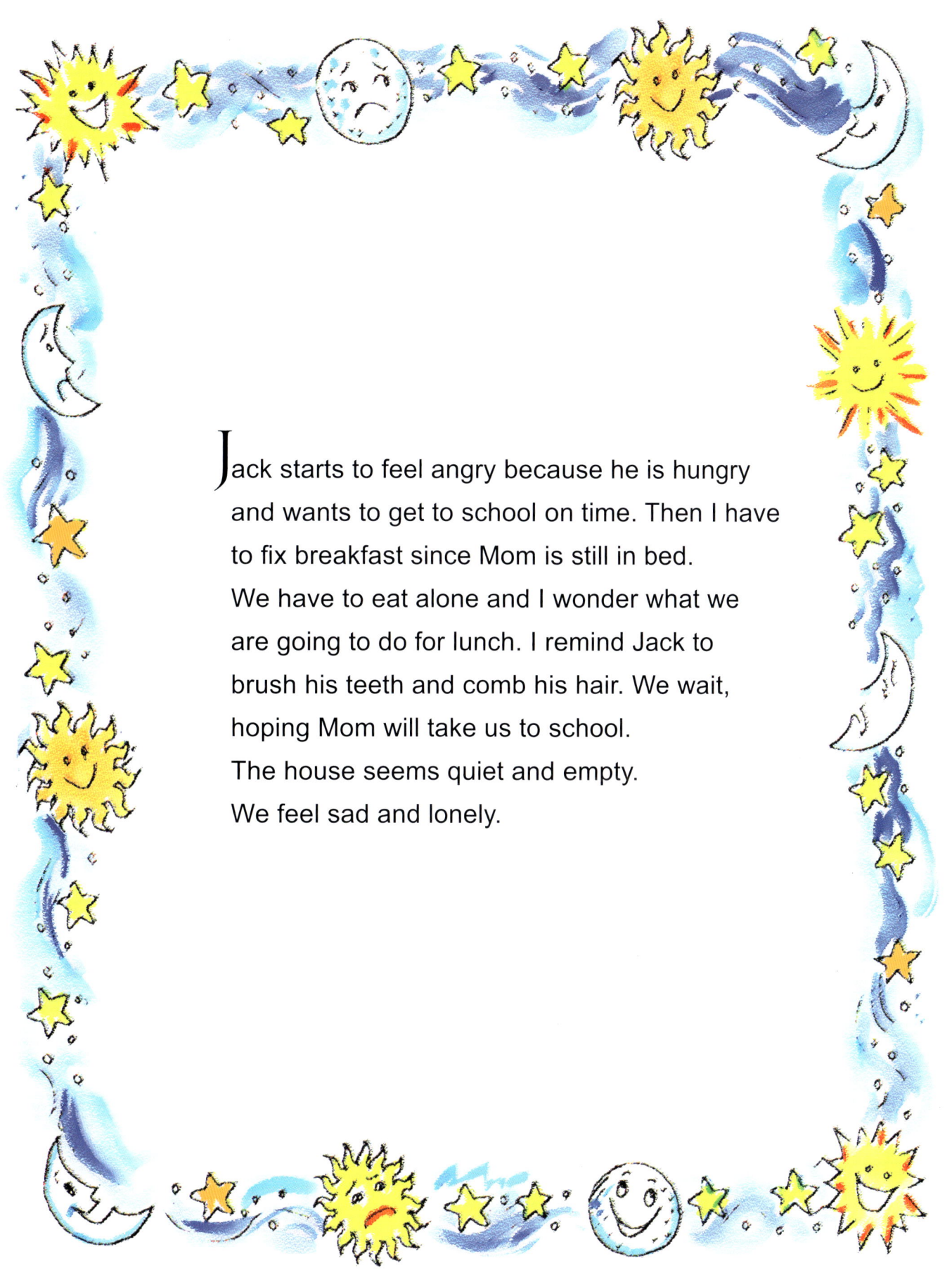

Jack starts to feel angry because he is hungry and wants to get to school on time. Then I have to fix breakfast since Mom is still in bed. We have to eat alone and I wonder what we are going to do for lunch. I remind Jack to brush his teeth and comb his hair. We wait, hoping Mom will take us to school.
The house seems quiet and empty.
We feel sad and lonely.

Some days when Mom does not get out of bed we stay home and try to take care of her. Jack feels so upset and asks, "What is wrong with our Mom?" I try to comfort him by saying, "She is not herself…but she will get better." Sometimes we don't know what to do about Mom. We are afraid to leave her alone. Before we had to move, our Mom would tell us to call Aunt Cheryl for help. She would come over and check on Mom. Then she would fix our lunches and take us to school. We want to go to school but we still feel worried and afraid.
What if our Mom needs us?

Sometimes when we come back from school we notice Mom is different. Like magic, her mood changes! (A mood is one kind of strong feeling and it can last for a long or short time).

We come home and the house is clean. Mom is playing her favorite music and the house smells yummy because cookies are baking. Mom seems happy and so are we!

Aunt Cheryl stays for dinner. We play games together, eat ice cream and have a great time! We feel loved and taken care of.

When Mom is in this good mood she likes to take us on a long car ride to the beach. We play together until the sun goes down. We have a special time together and we want it to last forever!

On the drive home, Mom is excited and talks a lot and makes all kinds of promises to us. She apologizes for staying in bed and ignoring us.

But sometimes this good mood scares us. Mom talks too much about all the good times she is planning for us and she drives too fast. All of this scares us because we do not feel safe. We also wonder how long this good mood will last.

Then, the next morning, without any warning Mom's mood changes. She is in a bad mood and gets angry at the smallest things.
Then she goes back to her room and goes to bed, just like before.

We wonder why… and if we did something wrong?
We feel confused and do not know how long this bad mood will last.
What is wrong with our Mom?

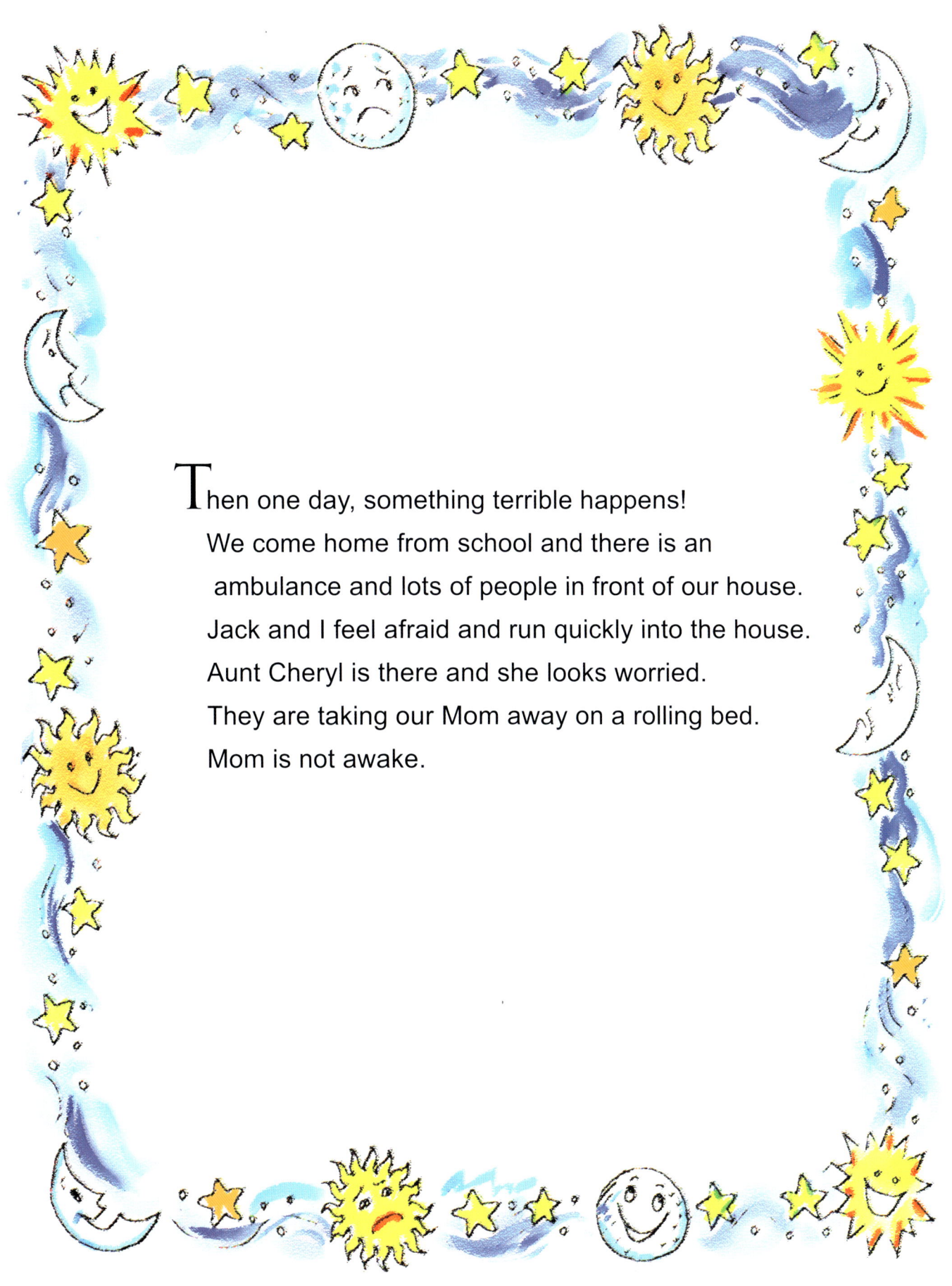

Then one day, something terrible happens!
We come home from school and there is an ambulance and lots of people in front of our house.
Jack and I feel afraid and run quickly into the house.
Aunt Cheryl is there and she looks worried.
They are taking our Mom away on a rolling bed.
Mom is not awake.

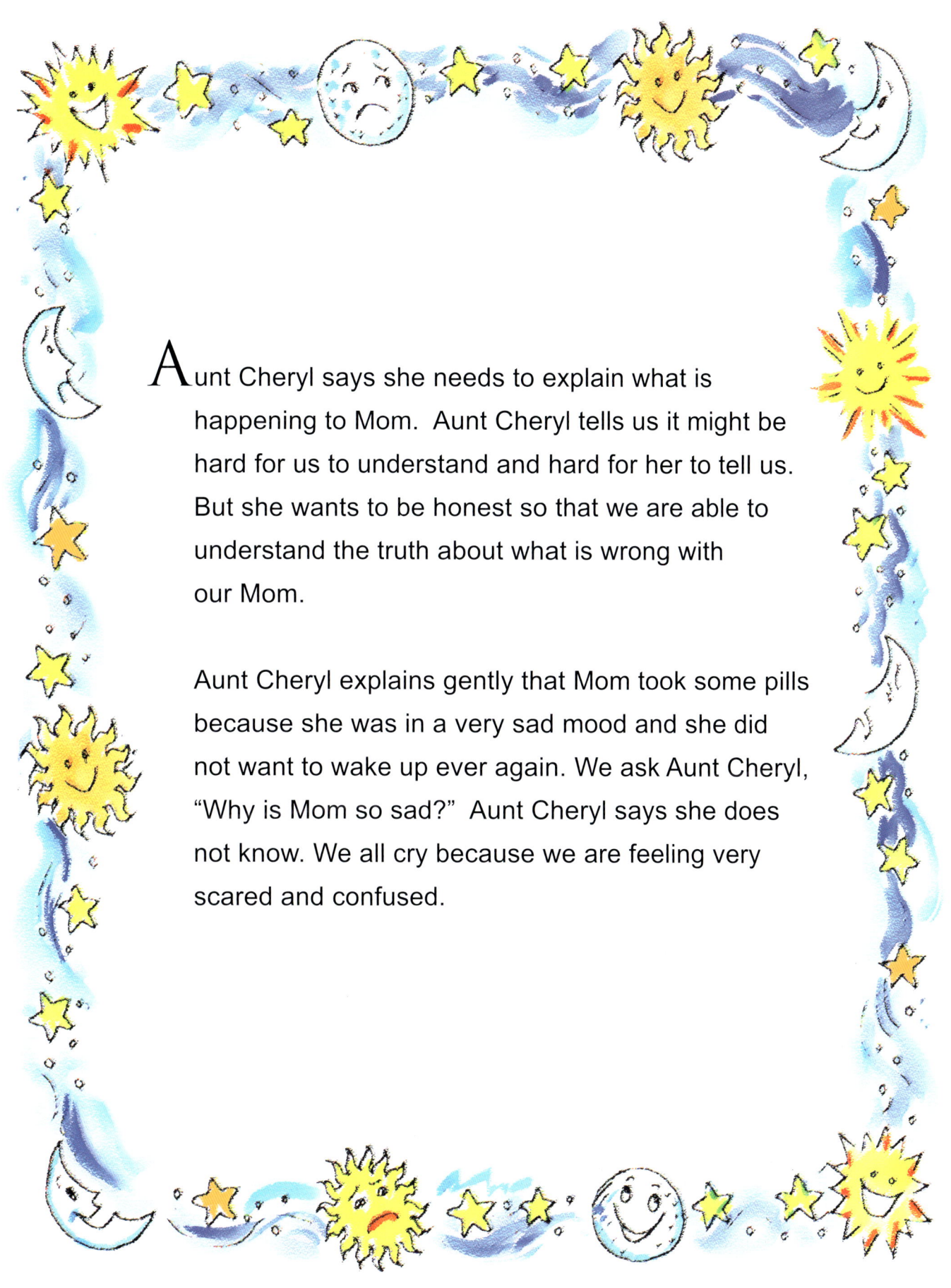

Aunt Cheryl says she needs to explain what is happening to Mom. Aunt Cheryl tells us it might be hard for us to understand and hard for her to tell us. But she wants to be honest so that we are able to understand the truth about what is wrong with our Mom.

Aunt Cheryl explains gently that Mom took some pills because she was in a very sad mood and she did not want to wake up ever again. We ask Aunt Cheryl, "Why is Mom so sad?" Aunt Cheryl says she does not know. We all cry because we are feeling very scared and confused.

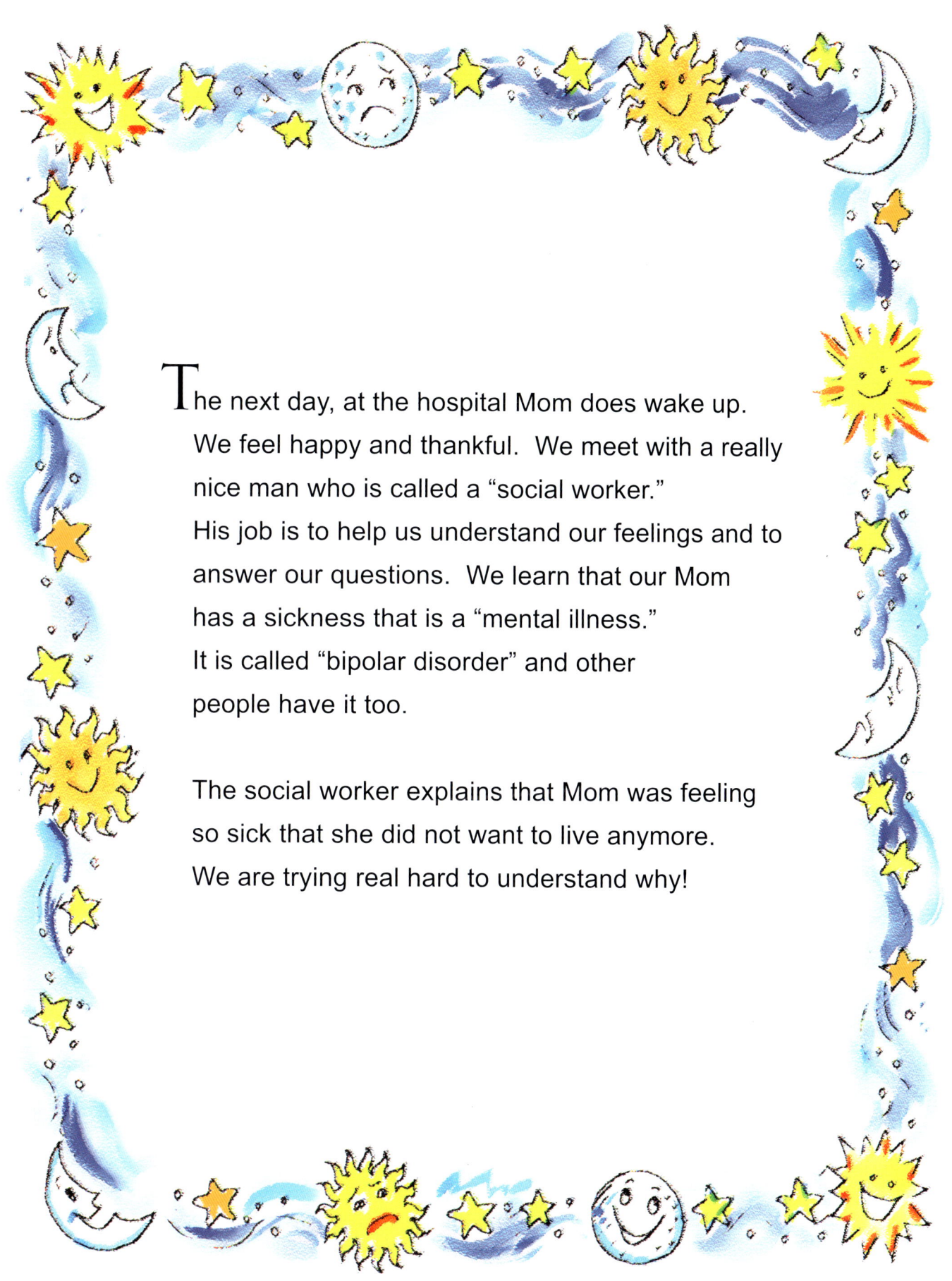

The next day, at the hospital Mom does wake up. We feel happy and thankful. We meet with a really nice man who is called a "social worker."
His job is to help us understand our feelings and to answer our questions. We learn that our Mom has a sickness that is a "mental illness."
It is called "bipolar disorder" and other people have it too.

The social worker explains that Mom was feeling so sick that she did not want to live anymore. We are trying real hard to understand why!

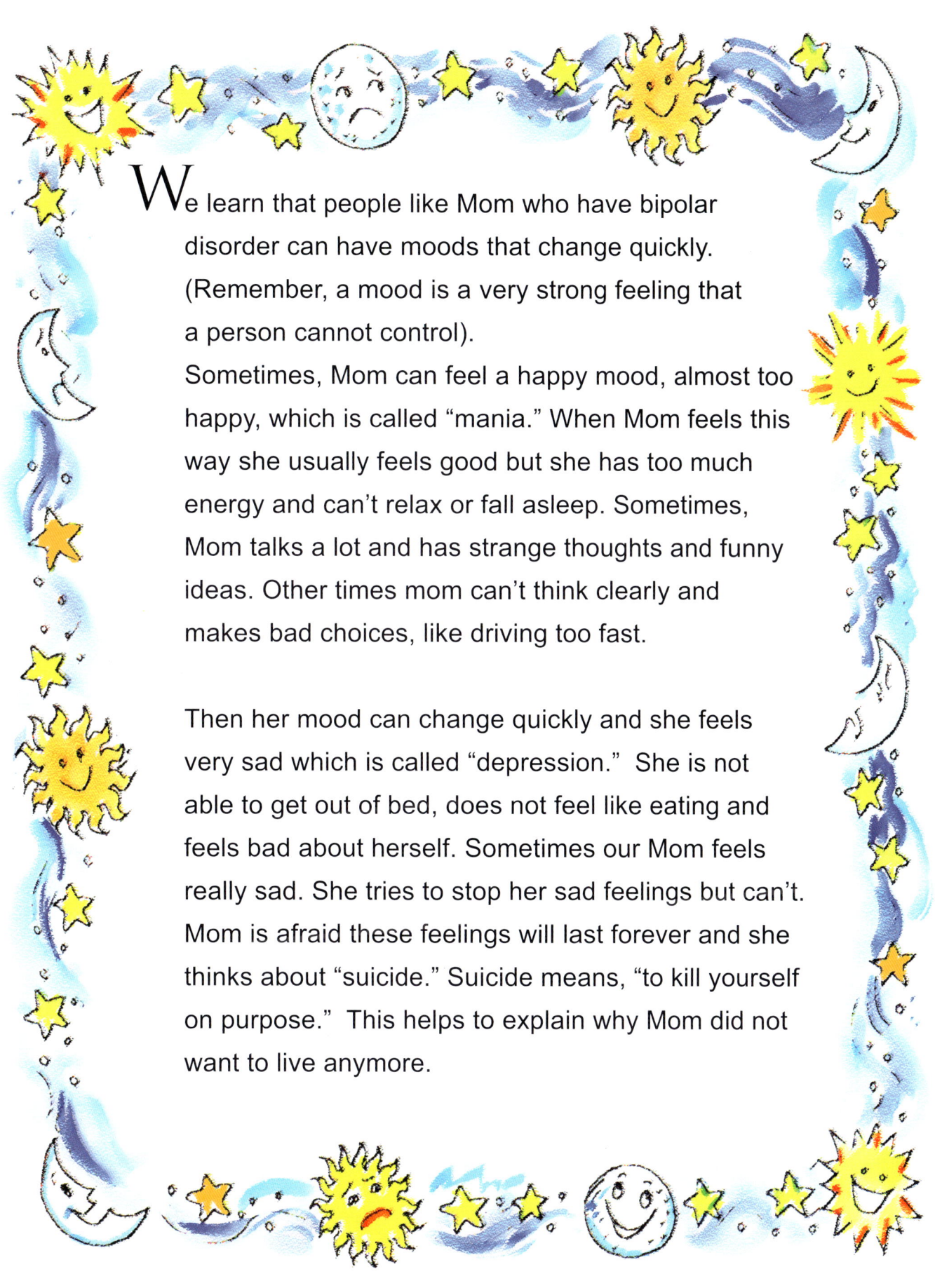

We learn that people like Mom who have bipolar disorder can have moods that change quickly. (Remember, a mood is a very strong feeling that a person cannot control).

Sometimes, Mom can feel a happy mood, almost too happy, which is called "mania." When Mom feels this way she usually feels good but she has too much energy and can't relax or fall asleep. Sometimes, Mom talks a lot and has strange thoughts and funny ideas. Other times mom can't think clearly and makes bad choices, like driving too fast.

Then her mood can change quickly and she feels very sad which is called "depression." She is not able to get out of bed, does not feel like eating and feels bad about herself. Sometimes our Mom feels really sad. She tries to stop her sad feelings but can't. Mom is afraid these feelings will last forever and she thinks about "suicide." Suicide means, "to kill yourself on purpose." This helps to explain why Mom did not want to live anymore.

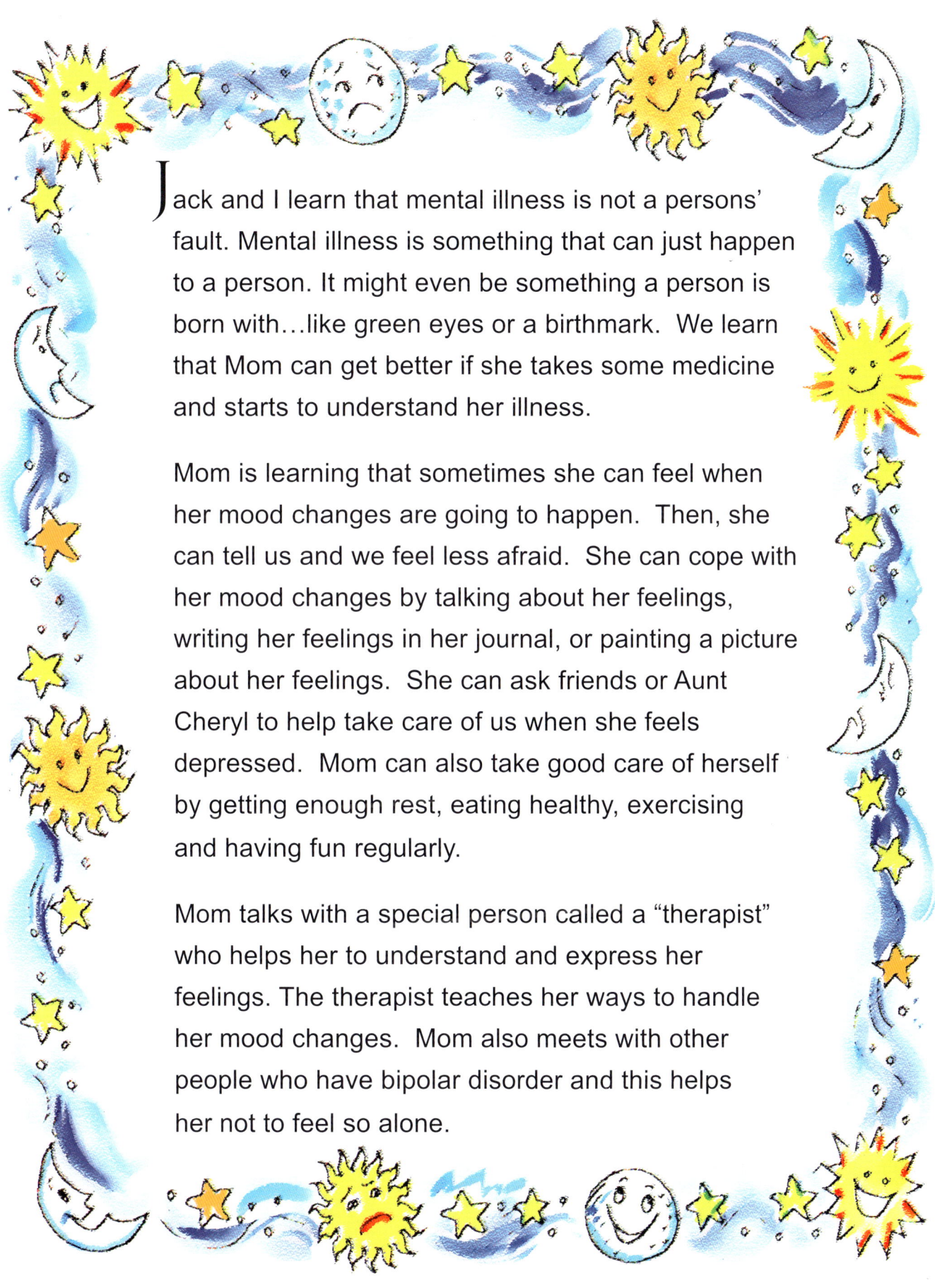

Jack and I learn that mental illness is not a persons' fault. Mental illness is something that can just happen to a person. It might even be something a person is born with…like green eyes or a birthmark. We learn that Mom can get better if she takes some medicine and starts to understand her illness.

Mom is learning that sometimes she can feel when her mood changes are going to happen. Then, she can tell us and we feel less afraid. She can cope with her mood changes by talking about her feelings, writing her feelings in her journal, or painting a picture about her feelings. She can ask friends or Aunt Cheryl to help take care of us when she feels depressed. Mom can also take good care of herself by getting enough rest, eating healthy, exercising and having fun regularly.

Mom talks with a special person called a "therapist" who helps her to understand and express her feelings. The therapist teaches her ways to handle her mood changes. Mom also meets with other people who have bipolar disorder and this helps her not to feel so alone.

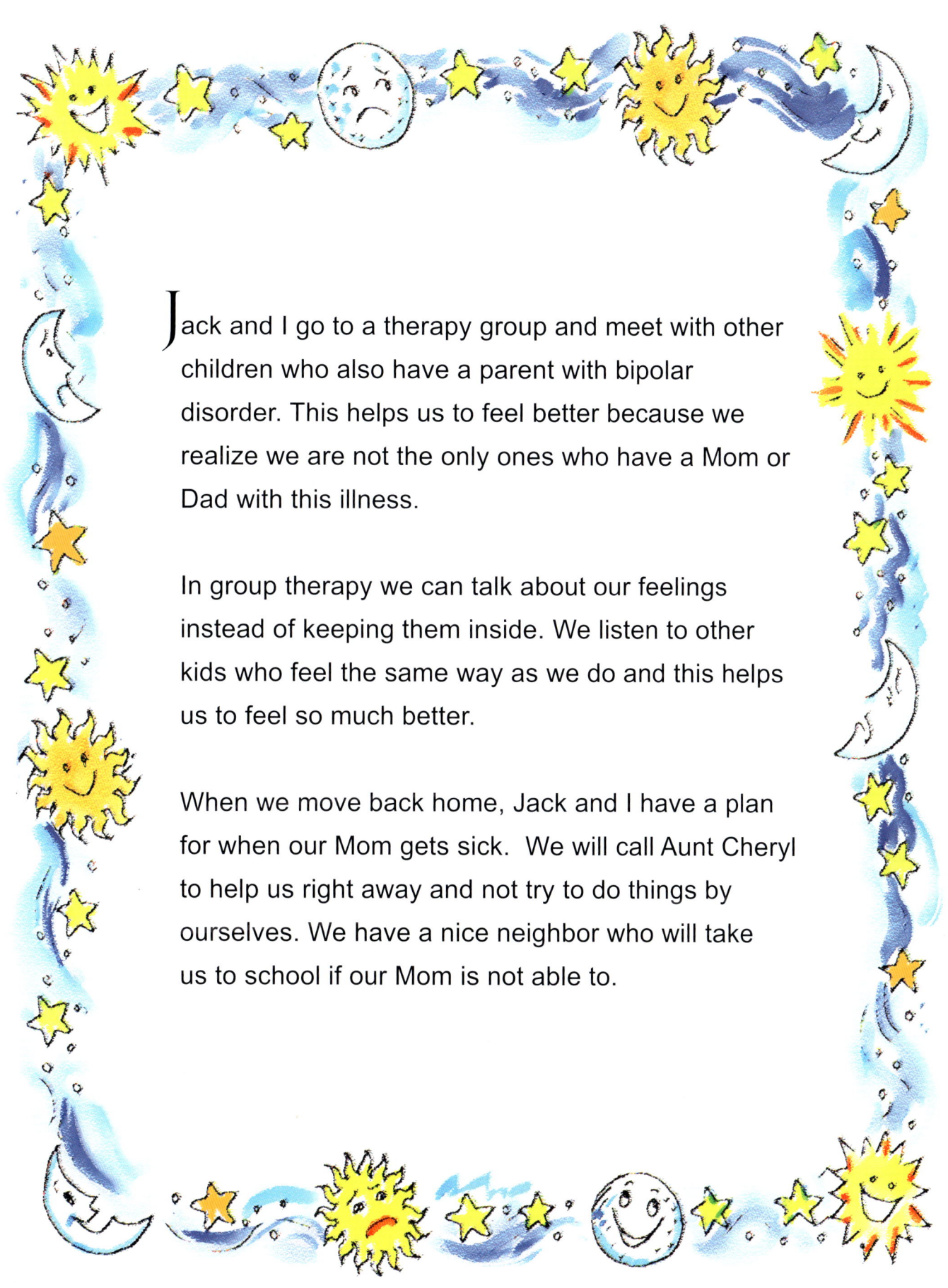

Jack and I go to a therapy group and meet with other children who also have a parent with bipolar disorder. This helps us to feel better because we realize we are not the only ones who have a Mom or Dad with this illness.

In group therapy we can talk about our feelings instead of keeping them inside. We listen to other kids who feel the same way as we do and this helps us to feel so much better.

When we move back home, Jack and I have a plan for when our Mom gets sick. We will call Aunt Cheryl to help us right away and not try to do things by ourselves. We have a nice neighbor who will take us to school if our Mom is not able to.

Jack and I are talking with each other about our feelings and I like to write my feelings in a journal book. Jack likes to draw pictures about how he is feeling. We can talk about our feelings with our new friends in group therapy because they really understand what we are going through. All of this helps us feel so much better!

Mom, Jack and I, all go together to a family therapist who helps us talk about our feelings. We share our fears, hopes and dreams for our family. We will soon be back together with our Mom in our own home but for now we are thankful to be living with our Aunt Cheryl. We are happy our Mom is getting help and feeling better.

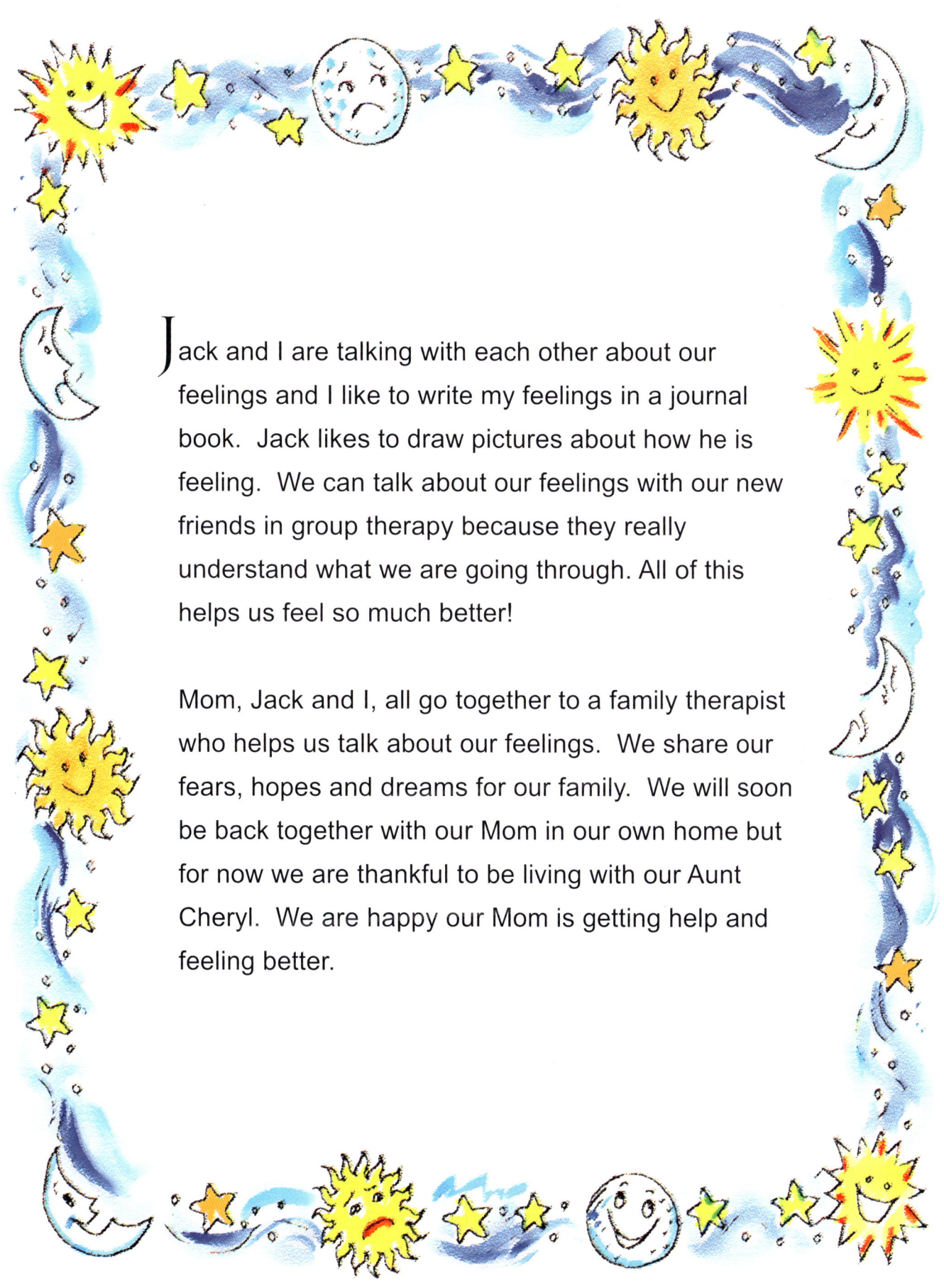

For now, Mom is living in a special home where she is getting the help she needs. She lives with other people who have different mental illnesses and they all work together to get better. Jack and I visit Mom every weekend and talk with her on the phone everyday. It is hard to be separated from our Mom because we love her so much, but we know it is not forever.

So for now, we are happy to be living with Aunt Cheryl. We feel safe and hopeful. We are learning a lot and so is our Mom. Even though Mom is not ready to come home yet, she is getting better and smiles more often. All of us are getting the help we need. We are looking forward to being together as a family again…real soon.

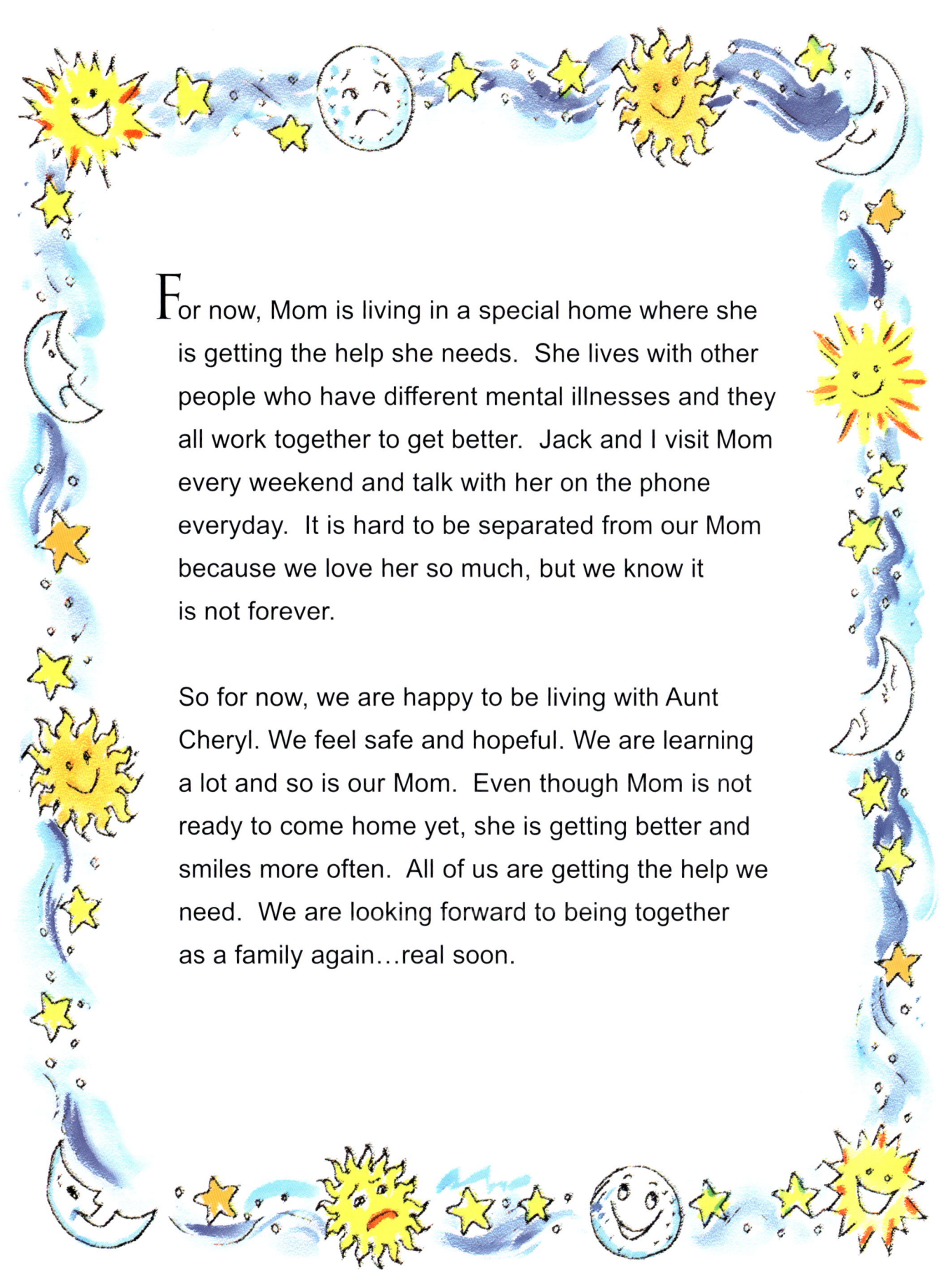

Resources: Bipolar Disorder and Depression

Child & Adolescent Bipolar Foundation

1187 Wilmette Ave., P.M.B. #311, Wilmette, IL 60091

www.bpkids.org

Depression and Bipolar Support Alliance

730 N. Franklin St., Suite 501, Chicago, IL 60610-7224

http://www.dbsalliance.org

The National Alliance for the Mentally Ill (NAMI)

Colonial Place Three, 2107 Wilson Blvd., Suite 300

Arlington, VA 22201-3042

www.nami.org

National Depressive and Manic-Depressive Association

www.ndmda.org

Moodswing

www.moodswing.org

Suggested Reading

Carter, Rosalyn, with Susan K. Golant. *Helping Someone with Mental Illness: A Compassionate Guide for Family, Friends, and Caregivers.* New York: Times Books, 1998.

Jamison, Kay Redfield. *An Unquiet Mind.* New York: Knopf, 1995; *Night Falls Fast: Understanding Suicide.* New York: Knopf, 1999

Mondimore, Francis Mark. *Bipolar Disorder: A Guide for Patient and Family.* Baltimore: John Hopkins University Press, 1999

Papolos, Demitri F., and Papolos, Janice. *The Bipolar Child.* New York: Broadway Books, 2002

Solomon, Andrew. *The Noonday Demon: An Atlas of Depression.* New York: Scribners, 2001.

Wolpert, Lewis. *Malignant Sadness: The Anatomy of Depression.* New York: Free Press, 1999.

Yapko, Michael D. *Hand-Me-Down Blues: How to Stop Depression from Spreading in Families.* New York: St. Martin's Griffin, 1999